Clint Faraday
#24
Death Walks Beside Me

Clint is in the mountains when he comes upon a very sad man. He asks why he is so sad, the man replies, "Because death is walking beside me."

What the hell does that mean? At the moment, Clint is walking beside him!

Contents

About the author

CD Moulton has traveled extensively over much of the world both in the music business, where he was a rock guitarist, songwriter and arranger and in an import/export business. He has been everything from a bar owner to auto salvage (junkyard) manager, longshoreman to high steel worker, orchid grower to landscaper, tropical fish farmer to commercial fisherman. He started writing books in 1983 and has published more than 350 books as of January 1, 2023. His most popular books to date are about research with orchids, though much of his science fiction and fantasy work has proven popular. He wrote the CD Grimes, PI series, and the Det. Nick Storie series, Clint Faraday series, and many other works.

He now resides in Gualaca, Chiriqui, Panamá, where he writes books, plays music with friends, does research with orchids and medicinal plants. He has lately become involved in fighting for the rights of the indigenous people, who are among his closest friends, and in fighting the extreme corruption in the courts and police in Panamá.

He offers the free e-book, *Fading Paradise*, that explains what he has been through because of the corruption.

CD is the discoverer of the Chadam Protocol for curing cancer.

Facebook page Ambrosia peruviana for cancer.

Death Walks Beside Me

A Beautiful Day

Clint Faraday, retired detective from Florida, woke up at his regular time, 5:00AM, and went to the kitchen to turn on the coffee maker, then to the bathroom for the regular routine, then out on his deck over Saigon Bay, Isla Colón, Bocas del Toro, Panamá, to watch the sunrise. It was going to be a beautiful day. The regular rain wouldn't come until late in the afternoon.

He had gotten used to the fact it rained a lot in Bocas del Toro. It was a coastal rain forest area. One of his favorite gripes was because people came to a tropical rain forest – and complained because it rained.

Well, DUH! What's your IQ? Minus ten?

Seven years here, and he'd heard that crap at least once a week in the rainy season, which was almost year around. It *is* a rain forest area. Get over it or get out!

He laid back in the hammock to sip the strong coffee. The light was breaking. The colors were striking. There were clouds out past Isla Solarte that were a glowing gold, with hints of salmon-pink and red. There was a slight breeze coming off the Caribbean to keep the day cool.

It would be a good day to go to the mountains. He hadn't been to see his Indio friends between Almirante and Chiriqui Grande in a few weeks. He wanted to see the clinic that was just finished he and some friends had built. The school was doing well, on the comarca, as was the one on Isla San Cristóbal.

That was one thing he was able to accomplish here. His cases brought in unexpected and large sums he could use for such purposes. Since coming to Panamá, his philosophy and viewpoint had changed. He was no longer earning money for the sake of Clint Faraday and earning money. That was an empty life, and held no emotional or psychological rewards. Many of his friends from the states or Europe had come to the same conclusions: Was that what your life was about? Was that the legacy you wanted to leave to your progeny? "He made a lot of money, then died?" Why not leave something they could point at with pride, and say, "My father (grandfather, etc.) built that! He did that kind of thing a lot!"

Clint could have them say, "He was also the second person ever to be declared a Ngobe!" That was a point he could point to with pride.

He could look in the mirror when he shaved, meet the eyes directly, and say he hadn't ever done anything to harm another person that wasn't in self-defense or in defense of his friends. He knew too many who never met the eyes in the mirror. He felt they would have to say, "I'm a piece of shit!" if they did.

Weird thoughts!

Judi Lum, his attractive neighbor, came out on her deck to water the orchids. She wagged a finger at him. That was a ritual, also. He didn't bother to put anything on until he decided what he was going to do that day. Judi had become a major part of his detective work here in Panama. He had never met anyone who could find information so fast. She would act like she wasn't in the least interested in a subject she mentioned in passing, so the person she was talking to would say something that she didn't seem to even hear. That meant they would repeat it, and stress it. They weren't careful about it, because she seemed so uncaring about the subject. Clint had tried the method, with limited success. Judi was as smart as anyone, but could act the total airhead.

Whatever. "Want to go to the mountains?" Clint called across. She answered that she was going to Changuinola with some friends. He waved and dove into the bay, swam around for fifteen or so minutes, got out, showered, dressed, got his boat, and headed for Tierra Oscura. He would leave the boat there and go into the mountains, then go across the carretera and up into the comarca. He might stay the night or several there with friends.

The water was slightly choppy, but that was this time of year. It wasn't bad. He stopped twice to greet his Indio friends in their cayucas, and to exchange news, then continued to tie to the little dock at a friend's place in Tierra Oscura. He chatted awhile with Nilsa, the wife of Arturo, his friend. They were Ngobe, and had two sons and a beautiful daughter who was just nineteen years old the week before. Nilsa said she and Arturo had something to discuss with him. It concerned Tyna, the daughter.

It wasn't long before lunch time, so Clint said he would return in about an hour, and they could talk. He went into the mountains to speak with other friends, and returned to find Arturo was home, as was Tyna. Nilsa had cooked a delicious fish lunch. They ate, then went out on the porch to talk. Arturo started.

"Clint, you are our very good friend and are a Ngobe. We wish for you to marry our daughter.

"I know how you feel about these things, but swear to you, it is her wish. She came to us. It will be a marriage in the old Ngobe tradition."

"Tyna has spoken to me often about you. She

has never been with another man until you tell her you will not agree," Nilsa said seriously. "You know how serious this is when one of our women will not.... She wants your answer."

Clint was shocked. He was old enough to not look for a wife and children, yet he had thought about progeny, just this morning. Tyna was a truly beautiful girl, and was much more than average intelligent. A Ngobe marriage lasted only as long as both partners wanted it that way. Many stayed married for life, though almost as many would declare divorce. The woman took the children. It was up to those children, after twelve years of age, to decide who was their father and who was their Papá. They would use the name of the biological father, but only under certain conditions. Often, the biological father was also the one they called Papá.

It was complicated. Clint wasn't at all certain he understood it completely.

"Tyna, is this true?" he asked.

"Clint, I have always loved you. I want my children to be with you. You will be a very good father, I know. I truly want this.

"I know this is serious. I will wait for your answer. I know it cannot be today."

"We also want this, Clint," Arturo said. "You are strong and intelligent. Tyna is strong and intelligent. It will mean strong and intelligent children. Please say that you will consider this request seriously."

"I promise you that. It is time I had a child to carry my name. I will give you an answer when I return from the mountains."

They didn't mention it again. They would wait for him to answer. Arturo was cutting nispero, and went back to work. Tyna went to help at the school. Nilsa was doing the housework, so he said he would return the following day or the next, most probably.

"Your answer will be yes, won't it?"

He considered a bit, then, "I think so." He went to the road and caught a ride to the carretera, then crossed and followed a stream-bed up into the mountains, crossed to the next mountain and was about where the comarca began when he saw a man sitting on a rock The man was about thirty or thirty five years old, and looked like a gringo or gringo Latin mix, and was in good physical shape. Clint got the impression the man had been crying.

He went to introduce himself, and ask why he was here in the mountains.

"I'm Vincent Lasko. Vince. I came up here to think about my life and ask if it was worth living anymore.

"You are going into the comarca? Will we be allowed? Some say it's dangerous, but I don't care about that. I need to see the differences in the culture. I need to consult with ... someone."

"I'm a Ngobe. It's alright to go into the comarca, unless the people have told you you're persona non grata. It's not dangerous to honest people. I'm Clint Faraday."

He nodded. "If I may walk with you?"

"Okay by me!"

They went through the little marker fence, and Clint asked, if it was any of his business, who he wanted to see on the comarca, and why was he contemplating suicide?

"Suicide? No! That's not what I meant. I only meant that I will have to ... death is walking beside me."

"What the hell does that mean?! *I'm* walking beside you!"

"I don't think there's any actual danger to you. I just used the expression because it was ... I was reading a murder mystery, one of the CD Grimes things. He was on an island, looking for someone, because of a series of deaths in the states. He met a Jamaican witch woman there who used the expression. She said that death was walking beside him, which mean it wasn't stalking him or something such.

"Death is walking beside me. I get to be friends with someone, and they end up dead. It can't be coincidence, and two of them were definitely murdered. The others seemed to have died in accidents or from natural causes. I want to talk with the witch woman or whatever they have on the comarca to see if there's some kind of curse or something on me. I meant that life isn't much worth the effort when you dare not have friends."

"Hmm. I don't much believe in curses, but I've seen things that can't be explained. If some were definitely murdered, it's not about a stupid curse. There's a specific reason someone is killing people you may be telling or showing things. That would have to be it.

"Have the deaths been in other than the states?"

"Yes. In Canada and Sweden. Germany. One in Hawaii, but that's the states. Two in Mexico."

"How long has this been going on!?"

"There have been eleven deaths I know of. It's been going on since I was about fourteen, believe it or not. That's why I think it must be some kind of curse. Nineteen years, it's been going on."

"Well, that gives us a puzzle! What happened when you were fourteen?"

"That's just it! I've tried to think of anything that happened before the first one – which was the first definite murder. There's nothing out of the ordinary!"

"What you think is the first one may not have been. It could be from earlier. Were there any deaths among your friends before that? Strange accidents, or whatever?"

"No. Well, a girl I played with a lot. She was hit by a car when she ran out in front of it. Annette. Before that, well, no. A boy I knew drowned, but he was with his family, and they were all together. He was a little strange, for ten years old, but we were friends, of sorts. He was, I don't know, horny all the time. At ten years old! We talked about sex a lot, but it didn't interest me much, at that age. I was just a little curious, but he had done a lot of things."

"Then something is very strange, and I tend to think it may have come from that time," Clint mused. "We can talk about it later. Here's the village."

They came into a little valley where there were a dozen or so of the Indio houses. Some children saw them, and ran out to hug Clint and call him abuelo (Grandfather) or tio (uncle). Clint asked if Madelena was around. They said she was helping a woman who was having a baby. She would probably be around a little later.

Clint introduced Vince to everyone, and said he had to speak with Madelena, so would come back in the morning. It was getting late, so they would find a place to spend the night. Several said they could stay with them. Clint said the parents would have to be asked. They went with Geraldo, who said they had a whole room no one was using now, that his sister went to live with her boyfriend.

They spent the night in the room. Clint had brought some food from Tierra Oscura they made a delicious meal of. Clint, Vince, and the family talked into the night, they went to the stream for a cold bath, then turned in.

In the morning Clint found that Madelena was back home, so took Vince to meet the medicine woman. She said she had a little power to read when there was a spell on anyone, and there was none on Vince or Clint, but there was something vague about Vince. Spirits that wanted to tell him something, but they were far away, and she didn't have the power to talk with the dead. She only could get one name that may not even be a name.

Landrow.

Vince looked a bit shocked, for a fleeting second, but said he thought it may be the name of a place, not a person. They thanked Madelena. She said Clint was about to undergo a very big change in his life. He was going to be a proud father in less than a year.

Clint looked even more shocked, and asked how she knew.

"I can lie and say the spirits told me, or I can tell you that Tyna wanted me to give her a potion or spell to make you fall in love with her."

"But you know I'll marry her?"

"She is beautiful, strong, clean, and smart. Those are what you want in your woman. She wants you. What's to figure in that?"

Clint laughed and hugged her. "Tell her your spell worked. I wasn't completely sure I'd go through with it until you told me she came to you. It's real. I think I can be happy with her, and maybe I can make her as happy with me. The age difference isn't important, here. It's the thing that could cause problems later, but I don't think it will."

"Ha! That will make many other women un-happy," she warned. "You are very popular. Not all are fellow Ngobe."

"They can eat their hearts out!"

Vince and Clint spent most of the day visiting with people and looking over the school and clinic construction, then headed back, with time to get to Clint's boat before dark. They stopped at Arturo's and made arrangements for Clint and Tyna to be married on the following day.

They headed for Bocas Town, just after dark. Clint knew the bay very well, and didn't have any trouble, even though it was raining steadily. Vince would stay in Clint's guest room. Clint was intrigued by this one. What had happened when Vince was nine or ten years old that had resulted in a series of murders? What did he know? Why were his friends murdered, when killing him would seem the more logical way to handle whatever it was?

That told Clint Vince had something. Not just something in his mind, something solid. A physical item. He probably didn't know what it was. Tomorrow, after the wedding ... well, the day after tomorrow, they could try to find what it was. Clint was going to be a bit busy tomorrow.

They got in and Judi came over to ask about the comarca. Clint told her he was marrying Tyna. Judi said she figured that months ago. Tyna had told her she was going full out to get Clint.

She always had information before anyone knew it was going to be important information!

Just before they went to bed, Clint remembered the shocked look on the comarca, so asked, "What's with Landrow? You very definitely reacted to that!"

"I don't *know*! All I know is that was the name of the first one. The sexy ten year old buddy! Landrow Morgan. My reaction was because, until that moment, I never really believed anyone had those powers. I hadn't even thought about him for fifteen years, at least!

"Clint, *how* did she come up with that name?"

"That's why I can't totally discount the tales

about the powers. If it had been Bill or Tom or John and an unclear initial, she would possibly have been fishing. Landrow? Uh-uh!

"What we have to face is that Landrow's been trying to tell you something for years. It will be what the murders were about, you can bet.

"Let it rest for awhile, now. We'll go over every detail you can recall, but don't think about it anymore than you have to. That drives things deeper, more often than not. I have someone who can make you remember things."

That was true! Living right next door!

They went to bed.

Clint wondered what Vince's reaction would have been if he'd been sleeping with one of the Indios. They would wrap up in you to share the body heat, at those altitudes. Clint always carried heavier blankets, so they didn't sleep together. Clint remembered the first few time he'd slept with an Indio, and grinned to himself.

Then again, maybe Vince would have enjoyed it. Clint didn't know or care, except for a mild curiosity.

In the morning Clint got dressed earlier than usual, but that was because he knew what he was going to be doing today. Vince said he would move into a hotel, but Clint said he could stay there. Vince argued that it was going to be Clint's honeymoon. He would want some privacy. Clint thought about it, and had to agree. This wasn't some pretty girl he'd just met who was going to spend a night or two.

"I have a friend who's not here for a few days. You can stay at his place."

He called Dave, his nutty musician/botanist friend, and made the arrangements. Dave said there was stuff in the refrigerator that would be dangerous to eat, now. Throw it out. Vince would have to buy his own food, and had *better* not let Dave come home to a sink full of dirty dishes. Clint told him he was getting married today.

"To Tyna? Judi told me it was coming soon. Congrats. Don't name any of your kids after me. Life's hard enough for them without that!"

Clint laughed and gave the phone the finger. He took Vince to Dave's apartment and moved him in. He would be on his own for the rest of today.

Then he headed for Tierra Oscura and his soon-to-be wife. He was amazed at how casual he was about it, but that's the Indio way. People got married if they wanted to raise a family. That was the way of the world. Out of a million men, nine hundred ninety five thousand or more would get married. Big deal!

Basilio was there, he was chief of the comarca, so performed what ceremony there was. He declared them married. That was it. Each could declare a special rule, which many did – for laughs. Clint said he'd stay married so long as she didn't get fat or interfere in his business. Fat turned him off. She said she would stay married until he turned into a drunk or started smoking or started giving her orders about the running of the house. Tobacco smells, and drunks turned her off. She ran the house, not him.

They went to Arturo's for a special lunch of chicken and rice, with a sauce Clint hoped Tyna knew how to prepare. They started with a chicken soup, much like Clint made, with otoe, potato, chayote, onion, celery, yuca, and garlic. It was delicious! For dessert, they went out on the porch and had guanabana chicha. Clint tried to figure what that meal would cost in a restaurant in the states and decided it would probably be less than a hundred dollars a plate, and wouldn't include the otoe or guanabana.

They went to Clint's place for the night. Judi came over when they got there "Just to be mean!" and brought some of her famous pineapple upside down cake.

The night was fantastic. For the first time in years, Clint didn't want to get out of bed to watch the sunrise – so he didn't. Tyna wasn't up at dawn to start the breakfast, either. They got up at what was a very late hour for both of them. 8:20AM, and showered together. Tyna cooked an omelet that tasted like pizza Romano and brewed some of the coffee her father dried and ground. It was rich and smooth.

Ben and Earl, a gay couple who lived a short distance toward Bocas Town, came by to offer their congratulations, then several other friends dropped in. Vince called and said he would wait until tomorrow to start their search. Clint would want to be alone with his new wife. Clint didn't argue the point. He would be like the gringos, on that point. The Indios didn't let such minor things as getting married disturb their regular work routines. Most people got married, and most people already knew what they needed to know about the sex part from the past fifty Saturday nights.

Clint and Tyna went into Bocas Town for the afternoon with Judi. They visited all the places Clint generally spent time, though Tyna wouldn't go to the bars alone, in the future. She liked the restaurants and shops, and would go with Judi when Clint wasn't around.

They went home at ten o'clock and went to bed. They got up earlier the next morning. 7:45AM.

The next morning, after canela pancakes and coffee, Clint called Vince and said they'd meet at the Golden Grill and decide where to go for the remembering session. Judi would be along. She was sort of a private secretary. There was some chemistry between Judi and Vince that Clint wondered about. It might be a help or hindrance.

Don and Jack were at the Grill. They waved, and Vince came in a few minutes later to sit at a table to the side. They chatted about the Indio culture and lifestyle. He thought maybe a couple of them were trying to pick him up. He asked if there were many homosexual Indios.

"Not strictly gay," Clint replied. "I would say a majority are bisexual, to one point or another. They don't think much about it. As Nica says, when you have an itch, what difference does it make which hand you use to scratch?"

"So I still don't know."

"You have blue eyes and are sort of classically handsome. They probably were. Blue eyes seem to be one of their biggest turn-ons. Nobody cares, here. It's up to you whether you take them up on it."

He shook his head. Judi came in and sat across the table. Clint asked where they should go to talk about some old murders. She said Vince was staying at Dave's, so why not there? They went.

"We'll start a little bit before you met Landrow," Clint suggested, when they were sitting at Dave's kitchen table with pineapple juice. "There had to be a time when he gave you something. Nothing else would make any sense. We'll have to know if anyone from that time seems to turn up in other places when you're there.

"Do you remember when you met him?"

"No, not really. We lived about three blocks away since I was about four or five, and would play cowboys and Indians and so forth. We did trade a lot of comic books and that sort of thing. He collected baseball cards. I remember that. I was more a football fan. He liked swimming and fishing. So did I. Even then, he was sort of an exhibitionist, I suppose. He would go outside naked to get clothes off the line and that sort of thing. He would take a leak against a bush when several of us were there.

"I remember him saying that a man was really handsome. Someone on TV. I agreed that he was handsome, but so were a lot of others.

"That was when he was about eight years old. He also would get really into some of the women he said were sexy, which the rest of us ignored.

"That was what we later called a classic molested child syndrome, wasn't it? I never thought about it, at the time.

"Anyhow, there's not very much about him I remember. He was just a friend I hung around with. He knew some really oddball people he would introduce me to, but they were older, and I didn't care to know them.

"Oh!"

"What?" Clint demanded.

"He had an uncle. They called him Ford. I don't know if that was his name, or just because he always had a souped up old Ford. He would take us ... it had to be him, didn't it? He took all the kids out to a little lake, skinny dipping, in the summer. He took pictures of us diving off a big rock. I hadn't thought about that in twenty years! He took pictures of everything. He carried three Polaroid cameras.

"I think ... I don't know. I think he felt us up a bit, at times, when he was drying us off when we went swimming. I never thought about it. One time I did think about what they told us in school about if some weirdo adult ever wanted to touch us 'inappropriately,' as they called it. I dismissed it, because he was Landy's uncle, and he was always there with us, and he didn't want us to get in the car wet.

"I can't think of any reason ... I didn't know anything about any of it. Other than those comics and baseball cards, he never gave me anything special that I remember."

"Then that definitely has something to do with it. Was Landrow particularly smart?"

"Come to think of it, yes. We made up jokes because he could always do math and stuff we couldn't."

"Were any others that went swimming among the ones who died?" Judi asked.

"Well, the girl, Annette."

"Did she die before or after Landrow?" Clint asked.

"About a week before. I remember thinking how terrible it was that two people I knew died in accidents in just one week."

"This is important," Clint said. "Have you seen Ford since that time?"

"Well, back home. They lived three blocks away. He wanted to take us swimming some more, but I told him it wouldn't be right without Landrow there. He was persistent, for a short time, and I wouldn't go. A couple of the other kids did. Sammy and Don, brothers, one ten and the other eleven. They went with him a lot. They were what we later called street toughs. Don was the older one. He got into some trouble and went to prison for stealing something ... a car. When he got out he was almost bragging about it. That was when he was nineteen or twenty. I don't know what happened to them. They moved.

"I remember something now! When I was thirteen or fourteen Sammy said he'd give me five dollars if I would let him fuck me! He said he really liked to fuck men. He always wanted to fuck me. I told him there was no way any guy would ever fuck me for any amount of money! He said he knew someone who had. I said he knew a liar, and I'd kick his smelly ass for him if he ever said anything like that about me.

"That would be Ford, huh? He was screwing all the young boys, and knew better than to mess with me. My father was pretty big. He didn't like any of the Morgans. He said they were trailer trash, and he wished I wouldn't associate with them.

"Looking back, I can't believe how blind I was! I was ten years old, which was why I didn't catch on, then, but I was fourteen and still never caught on!"

"Do you still have those baseball cards and comic books?" Judi asked.

"I suppose they're in the attic at the old house. My sister lives there, now. There's something in them, isn't there?"

"That's why death is walking beside you. He's afraid someone else will get the cards, or whatever it is, if anything happens to you. What's there has to be damned important!" Judi said.

"You're still alive because he thinks you have whatever it is, and kills anyone you might have given it to or shown it to, or something."

"But that can't be!" Vince cried. "There've been two deaths since he died! Ford's been dead almost three years. One murder was just five weeks ago!"

They decided to see if Vince could get his sister to send the box of stuff from the attic to him. He said everything like the baseball cards was in that box. It would cost almost two hundred dollars to have it airmailed to him overnight. Clint said he'd pay for it. Get that box!

All they could do now was wait.

The box would arrive on the Air Panamá flight at 4:30. It had been two days that Clint spent with his wife. She liked a lot of the same things he did, so they would live partly like gringos and partly like Indios. Clint couldn't think of anything that Vince could have that wouldn't have passed the statute of limitations. That meant whatever it was would hang someone for murder.

Ford was already dead. Who was continuing the killing? Why?

He could only hope he'd get an answer or two from the box.

Clint and Vince went to the airport to get the box. Aduana checked it and tried to hit them up for import taxes on valuable collector's items. Clint put a quick end to that. He worked with the police a lot, and the aduana man knew it. He said they weren't collector's items, they were evidence in a murder case. He could have Sergio, head of the police there, come to explain what could happen if they screwed around with the evidence in a criminal case. Clint showed him the forms he'd filed when the box arrived. It stated the box contained possible evidence in a multiple murder case.

They were passed through. Fast!

They took the box to the police station for Sergio and Emilio to observe their careful search through the items. There was a baseball signed by Willie Mays, which Clint said was probably worth a bundle, in itself. Vince said it was a forgery. Sammy used to do that a lot. He could copy a signature so close even the person it was supposed to be by couldn't be sure was a forgery. There were some old newspaper articles that had been cut out. There were a lot of photos, only a few were Polaroid. There were items that kids will collect. There was a fancy gold pendant watch in a box with "Annie" scratched into the back. The receipt was in the space under the velvet pasteboard in the box. It was made out to Thomas Arnold Longshire.

"Who was Thomas Arnold Longshire?" Sergio asked.

"I don't remember. Maybe the guy we called Tommie. He was some kind of politician who ... Jesus!" Vince exclaimed. "He went with us skinny dipping a few times! He and Ford were pals for years!"

"I don't get it?" Sergio asked.

"Annie – this is supposition – was nine years

old. She gets an expensive gift from an upwardly mobile politician. He goes skinny dipping with a bunch of kids and another person who was an apparent pedophile. The little girl ends up dead. There are a series of murders from that time to today that are centered around Vince, somehow. He had this stuff that one of the kids at the swimming parties gave him. That kid was, I think, murdered by his uncle, the pedophile.

"I think that kid had this and possibly more evidence in this box, and told his uncle he had it, believing it would keep him from having anything happen like what did. The holder of that box has a bunch of murders of anyone who became a closer friend."

"You think that Ford drowned Landy?" Vince asked.

"I think we have to know a lot more than we ever will, but yes. I think, just maybe, Landrow told Ford about the evidence while the family were enjoying a day at the beach. Landrow obviously knew how to swim if he was at those old skinny dipping parties. Ford panicked and drowned the kid, then realized he had no way to get the evidence. He also knew or felt that you didn't know you had the evidence, so it would be safe enough, unless and until you started going through those old things. Did Ford know you weren't interested in baseball?"

"Yeah. He took us to a couple of games where I was bored. He also knew I didn't care much for the comics, because he would buy them and I wouldn't even bother to read most of them, except a few Spiderman and Superman comics."

"So!" Sergio said, "now you have the things and won't ever bother to look at them – except you have friends who collect them you might give them to?"

"Well, a couple people asked about old comics and baseball cards when that little fad about collectable things was going for a few years. The late nineties. I always said there might be some of that in storage, then forgot about it."

"This is all too far out. It's supposition at the worst level, but might be close," Clint said. "We have to find what else is here and add it up."

"This should give you enough to pick this Ford character up on the pedophile charges," Emilio suggested. "You can probably tie the murders to him."

"He's dead," Vince replied.

"Then you've solved the case, anyhow," Emilio said.

"Except that the murders continued after he was dead," Clint pointed out.

"Shit!"

"It'll be that politician who bought the pendant for her," Sergio decided.

"He goes to several different countries to kill people while he's an elected official? I don't think so!" Vince fired back.

"Then we're missing something very important here," Emilio said.

"No kidding?" Clint replied. "We have to find a connection with someone else. I don't doubt for a second Ford killed Landrow and some others. Maybe that politician killed Annie. It's not all of this mess, but it takes away the reason to kill your friends when we have the box and we've seen everything.

"So let's see everything. Maybe it'll clear up by itself."

They went through the items without finding anything else, so they opened the several baseball card packages. There were a lot of passport-sized pictures of kids between the cards with the names on the back . They were taken with a Polaroid and cut to size. Vince was looking through the stack of twenty eight pictures when he suddenly cried, "Christ almighty!"

"What?" From Sergio.

"Elizabeth Carlington. She was one of the murdered people, less than a year after Annie and Landy."

Sergio wrote the names on all the pictures down and took them to the scanner to have copies made of all of them on a page. He then sent the pictures and names, along with the town, Lakefordhampton, South Carolina, to the police in South Carolina. "We'll start getting answers in a couple of hours, I hope."

"I hope. Answers are what we need," Vince said.

Clint was looking through newspaper clippings. He said that they were all about prominent state businessmen and some politicians. The Longshire character was running for Attorney General. His reputation was established as prosecutor for the county, and his record was exemplary. The picture was of a stern-looking man in his early thirties.

"I've found something!" Emilio cried. "There are photographs in the pages of the comic books! They're of children with adults, mostly. Some are pretty disgusting."

There were sixteen of those pictures. One was of Longshire and Annette. The names and dates were listed on the backs. Annette was nude, and Longshire had his pants down. The date was *April 6, 1987 – Annie and Tommie – the lake*.

Clint rapidly went back through the newspaper

articles to find an article about a little girl being hit by a car. April 6, 1987. The car was driven by Alice Downs. She said the little girl ran right out from the thick hedge in front of her, and she couldn't stop. A prominent citizen, Mr. Thomas Longshire, was nearby, and saw the accident. He stated that the girl ran out because her little dog ran out, and she was trying to catch it. The dog later returned to the home of the girl.

"So. He pushed her out in front of a car to shut her up about the pedophile bit," Sergio said. "He's still alive and is an elected official. *Him*, you can tag!"

"There's something more, but that's a given!" Clint agreed.

They matched the pictures of businessmen and the kids from articles with the photos taken from the comic books. They used magnifying glasses to check every least detail. The pictures were clear enough that they could see small things. Emilio noted, after studying six of them, that four of the men had a similar ring, friendship rings, they were called in the seventies and eighties. It was on the right ring finger. Silver setting with a very small catseye stone, as shown in one that had the ring shown with the man's hand on a Bible. He was shown being sworn in as a special deputy investigating vice issues in the town.

"I'm going to vomit!" Sergio declared. "If that ring means what I think it does, I'll want to see that bastard executed when the gas is so low it takes an hour for him to die!"

"That would be far too good for him," Clint agreed. "I think we'll find that all of them wear or wore that kind of ring. A ring that identified a pedophile ring.

"Vince, how did Ford earn a living?".

"I don't know. He always had money. I never

saw him do anything."

"I think it explains what the deaths are about," Clint said sourly. "I think someone in that ring was around every time someone died. I think they're taking turns watching Vince. I think they know he has this stuff, but don't have a clue as to how to get it. I think they believe he knows he has it and has an arrangement somewhere that it gets released if anything ever happens to him, directly."

"Well, most of what we're supposing here is stretching things. This is a wilder stretch," Vince said. "It gives me pause, because I've seen people I thought looked familiar, but couldn't connect anything to them. That Billings character, the one who owns the bank or whatever in the article, I recognize definitely as seeing in Germany, in Hamburg, and Gloria Friedman died there in a so-called accident when she fell from a scaffold while setting up an art exhibition. It was strange, because she wouldn't have died if she hadn't fallen head first onto a broken concrete block that just happened to be there.

"Gloria was a close friend. We dated now and again. I was there because of the exhibition."

"We have to get in touch with some of those children who were at the skinny-dipping parties," Sergio suggested. "It will be a problem, because they aren't in this country. I have received a great deal of information from the request with the pictures. I don't begin to know how to handle this international stuff, when none of it happened here! We can contact nine or ten of them."

"I'll see what I can arrange to get some of them here," Clint said. "All we need is one who has information, and will tell us about a few things."

"How will you manage that?" Vince asked.

"I'll use the mafia connection."

Sergio grinned. Emilio and Vince just looked confused. Clint went outside to use his celular. When he came back inside, ten minutes later, he said they would have to wait a few days, but something would be arranged. Sergio swore everyone there to complete silence. He locked the evidence box into a triple-locked cell. Those people had money, and he intended to see that no one got to that box.

Clint suggested that Vince enjoy a vacation, but be careful. If anyone suspected anything, they might think it was time to take a chance and knock him off. He would call when something was arranged.

He went home to his wife.

"Manny, did you find any of them, and were you able to get any of them to come here?" Clint asked Manny Matthews, formerly called Marko Bocinni, mafia boss from the US who had moved here to escape his reputation. He didn't want his kids to have to hide where Pops made his. He'd turned into quite a popular and helpful friend, particularly with the Indigenos. He lived on Isla San Cristóbal.

"I've got two women and one man in their early thirties, and one man in his sixties. I let them each learn that they had won a free all-expense two week stay for two in lovely Bocas Town, Isla Colón, Panamá. They're all the type who enter contests in the local papers and on the net and such."

"You got one of those big businessmen who enters contests?"

"Not all businesses make a lot of money. The ones in real estate are now reduced to begging quarters on the streets in the states, at the moment."

"When will they arrive?"

"Friday, Saturday, Sunday, and Monday. No two on the same flight."

"I owe you, Manny."

"Uh-huh. Half what that's going to cost. I pick up half."

They chatted for a few more minutes, then Clint called Sergio and said he'd be there to make the arrangements.

"Is the older one named Longshire, perchance?" Sergio asked.

"No. We couldn't hope to get anything like that. His name's Kestle. The one with that boy you had identified as Paul Owens. The other three are Kenneth Goode, Louise Canter, and Robert Dobbs. You have them identified, so we'll know who to watch as soon as they land in Panamá City."

"We're keeping a close eye on Haddon, too. He's not moving an inch we don't know about."

"Haddon?"

"Judi didn't tell you? She saw him in the Reef. He was talking to a couple of the street boys. He was buying them dinners."

"And?"

"He wears a cat'seye ring on his right ring finger."

"I'll be damned! I should have thought to look for that!"

"Judi did. She said you suggested it. You said they all wear that kind of ring."

"Our amazing information machine!"

"Well, I'll see you day after tomorrow at the airport when the Aeroperlas Panamá City flight lands. We can then wait for the Air Panamá flight Sunday, etc."

"I *will* be there!"

They chatted a few minutes, made their plans, then Clint called Judi. She said she thought he would want her to try to find those people. Haddon met with a man called Jerry every night at Toro Loco. They both were popular with the street kids, buying things from and for them. Jerry didn't wear the ring, that she saw.

"I don't much like that," Clint said seriously. "They're good kids."

"Oh, they know more about that kind of thing than those creeps. They know just how to use them."

"But that girl, Annie, ended up dead."

"It won't happen here. These kids know how to prevent it. I talked with Silvio and Niño about it, and they said they wouldn't let them do anything they didn't like. Silvio said there were fifty of them in the past few months who felt him up. Some of them did a bit more, when they had the money. They won't tell who or what, but they know more about that stuff than you and me added together. They're safe, as long as everyone knows they won't ever talk unless someone tries to force them to do something, then they'll just get fifteen or twenty of them together and kick hell out of anyone who gets too far out of line."

"That what happened to that Itallian guy on

Popa?"

"I think so. He was in the hospital for two weeks before he decided to move to the city."

Clint shook his head. It was true that these kids knew about almost anything that could happen to them, and knew how to handle it. The Indios would stick together, all the way. That's how they survived on the streets. The boys would set a price for whatever, but you didn't mess with the girls. Ever. Not until they were over twelve years of age, and then it was up to them if they didn't want any of that kind of life.

Well, it was all finally coming together, now. Clint wondered how he would react if his kids were as open. He didn't think they would be on the streets, to any extent, but he didn't lie to himself about what could happen when their best friends were mostly street kids.

He was an Indio, by declaration. Tyna was an Indio by birth. He was going to raise his kids the Indio way, to the greatest extent. You'd have to be blind to not see the difference in the Indio children and the Latinos and Blacks. You'd be a fool to want your kids to act other than the way the Indio kids acted.

This kind of thing made a father or soon-to-be father think.

He went home, then he and Tyna went to visit

her parents for the afternoon and evening. No sense in making plans about how to raise your children before you had them. Plans didn't often work out like you thought they would, anyhow.

Clint and Sergio lounged around in the terminal as the plane taxied to the concourse. The plane sat for a moment, then the port opened and the passengers began to deplane. Sergio said, "That's her!" when a somewhat flamboyant, slightly plump redheaded woman come down the steps. She came into the reception to claim her luggage, and they watched her. She went to the door where she handed a taxi driver a page, he put her stuff in back and headed for the Bocas del Toro Hotel. Sergio and Clint went to the hotel, arriving as she was getting out of the taxi. She went into the lobby with her paper to be given a room on the water. She went up and stayed a few minutes, then came back down and went to the restaurant to order a menu and a margarita. Clint was about to walk over to introduce himself when Sergio put a hand on his arm.

"What?"

Sergio pointd to a man who came into the restaurant just then. Clint raised an eyebrow.

"Jerrald Haines. The one Haddon meets."

Haines was strolling out toward the deck, and

came to a stop, staring at the woman.

"Lou?" he asked. "Imagine meeting you, here in Panamá! (He pronounced it "Panamamaw")"

"Jer?! What are you doing here?"

"Er, my vacation. I heard about it and decided, seeing I had a week or two, to see what it's like."

"You like the little chocolate girls – and boys – or the white ones?"

"Come on, Louise! That was a long time ago!"

"It was yesterday, if I know you! Sit! Have a drink!"

He sat. The waitress came over, and he ordered the chuleta. She said she didn't know what that was, but knew he was a gourmet, so ordered the same. He said it was a pork chop.

"Guess who else is down here," Haines said. "Francis."

"Well, you have someone to talk to. You would know, so tell me about the Indians. I hear they're really great for sex."

"The blacks have the reputation, but the Indios, as they call them here, run away with the title."

"The blacks have the reputation everywhere. They might be hung heavier, but they're usually lousy in bed. You wouldn't catch that. So long as they're not more than ten, they're perfect to you.

"I hear they'll hang you from the nearest tree if you mess with kids here."

"The girls, yes. You have to be very careful. I haven't found an Indio boy over six who doesn't know more than I do."

"You don't *know* anything. You just think you do."

"We shouldn't be talking about this here, Lou."

"They don't speak English, so why not?"

Clint grinned, and went over to say, "Because they all speak English. I'm Clint. Where are you from?"

"I'm Louise, just Lou. He's Jerry. We're from Lower Mudville, USA. Where are you from, handsome?"

"Florida. I'm from here, now. I'm a native. Ngobe."

"You're a native? From Florida? A whatever you said?"

"Ngobe are the Indios. You are *not* an Indio!" Haines said.

"Hi, Clint. Coin dere! Moga me dende?" Janeth, the waitress, said, as she brought the silverware and a pitcher of cold water.

"Oye, Janeth! Coin dere!"

"What was that?" Haines asked. "It sure as living hell wasn't Spanish!"

"Guayme, the local Indigeno language," Janeth answered. "Clint is Ngobe." She went back to the kitchen.

"This is one weird place," Louise said, grinning.

"Uh-huh. You're the really weird ones, here," Clint replied. "The chief declared me Ngobe. According to the constitution, all Ngobe are native Panamanians, so I'm a native.

"Well, I'll probably see you around! I have to get home to the wife!"

"Gringa or Latino or black?" Haines asked.

"Ngobe," Clint answered.

"Declared?" Louise asked, grinning.

"No From Isla Popa. Caio!"

He walked off. Louise looked smug. Haines looked very uncomfortable.

"Wait until Goode gets here tomorrow! I'll bet there's going to be some very hard questions asked!" Sergio declared.

"We have to protect Vince, Sergio."

"Yes. Emilio or Estefan are with him twenty four seven for the nonce."

Clint nodded, and went home to Tyna.

"He met Haddon, and they had a little conversation that included a lot of pointing and arm waving last night. Canter came in, and they were all buddy-buddy, although she very obviously doesn't think much of Haddon. She baits Haines, all the time, but a lot of it's good-natured. She flirts with anything in pants, including the women in pants." Sergio was reporting to Clint and Judi at the airport. "Her life isn't ruined from it, but she's definitely been changed. She just happens to be the kind who would have been a nympho, anyhow."

"I managed to be at the Bocas for breakfast, and she came in," Judi said. "She sat with me because I had the only table that had a place to sit with anyone who speaks much English. She asked a lot about you. I told her you were our local legendary character. You were a detective in the states, and work with the police here, sometimes. You really are a declared Ngobe, the second in history. You protect the Indios, and do a lot of work with them in education and medicine – and weren't you the sexiest thing since Elvis."

Clint gave her the finger.

"She said she tried to seduce you, but you have a wife. I told her you're Ngobe. You truly love your wife, and will protect her and provide, but you also will chase a piece of tail when the mood strikes you. That's how the Indios are.

"She said she didn't understand why you didn't go for her. I told her you like dark thin women. The selection is so much here, you can be choosy. We're neighbors, and things get too sticky if we have a thing, so we both avoid it.

"You said that about her saying the Indios were

supposed to be great in bed. I introduced her to Guillermo.

"I was prattling about all kinds of things."

"You are the consumate airhead!" Sergio stated. "At least, you can make people think you are. What did you learn?"

"That there are two men here who you'd better watch your little kids around. She knew them in the states. There are a lot of that kind there."

"To which you answered?" Sergio asked.

"Oh, look! I think I've seen that *gorgeous* man on the surfing team thing at Drago!"

"Who was he?" Clint asked.

"I don't have a clue. He looked like a surfer."

Sergio gave her the old middle finger. Nobody could act the ditzy airhead better than Judi, when she wanted information! "Here comes the plane. Here comes Goode."

They waited until a thin nervous man came aground, and watched as he went to pick up his luggage. He took a taxi to the Bahia, and went in.

"Haddon stays there, but he's on the tour boat to the Zapatillas with Vince and Estefan," Sergio said. "You don't have to say it. He's not going to have a chance to do anything."

Clint's phone buzzed. It was Tyna.

"Clint? Some man was just here asking a lot of questions about you and the police. I wouldn't let him inside, and buzzed the call thing to Ben. He and Earl came very soon, and the man left. He said he wanted to write an article about you in *The Traveler* or something. Earl said you already had ten or twelve articles about you there, and didn't care for anymore publicity. He left. Ben and Earl will stay here until you come home. Earl will cook that tuna you have in the freezer for dinner.

"Here's Ben."

"Clint? It was that Haines character you pointed out to me. He wasn't threatening or anything. He was just trying to get some information about you. We'll stay until you get home tonight, just to be sure."

"Thanks, Ben. I think maybe he was just trying to establish that he's here in Bocas Town, not on a boat tour somewhere. I'll have Sergio contact Estefan and warn him that something's up!"

He talked a bit more, then hung up. Sergio heard the conversation and called Estefan. Vince would be safe.

"Well, this pots getting warm. Let's see how fast we can make it boil!" Clint said.

"You're sick!" Judi shot back.

"Well, I guess I'll wander back to town to see what happened on the tour," Clint said, after the superb tuna steak dinner. "I want to be there when Haddon meets Goode! After Canter, nerves are going to be getting stretched pretty tight, I'd imagine."

"I agree," Ben said. "I think I also agree with Earl about your sick attempts at being poetic, or whatever. Don't! It's not w-o-r-r-k-i-n-g!"

Clint laughed and gave him the finger. He dressed a bit and headed to town. Sergio was sitting at the Golden Grill, so he sat across from him.

"Haddon's in the pisser. Goode's at the Lemon Grass. Canter's in her hotel with Guillermo, trying to wear him out, while he's probably more determined he's going to wear her out. Vince will accidentally meet Canter and Haines when it can be arranged. I'd like for Goode to be there, too."

"Things are getting hotter, Sergio. We have to protect Vince. I think he should visit Manny for a few days."

"I was going to suggest it. If they get desperate,

they could do something stupid and fatal."

They talked a few minutes more. Clint called Manny and made arrangements for Vince to go to the island. Manny said he had some information that may or may not be what this was about.

"It seems there is a band or club of some kind around a little town. Lakefordhampton. They're pedophiles who share little kids and such. They have some kind of identification sign or something. Some are supposed to be real big shits in business and politics.

"Help any?"

"The sign's a cat'seye and silver friendship ring worn on the right ring finger," Clint said. "We're connecting them to some murders in several countries. Here is supposed to be the next one, I think. We know who and why, so can send him to stay with you a couple of days, if you'll agree?"

"Certainly! I've got four rooms that aren't being used."

They chatted for a few minutes, then Clint hung up. He called Vince on the celular he'd given him and told him to go to his place. Tyna would take him to a friend's place. He'd explain later.

He told Estefan what was going on. Estefan would ride to Manny's dock with Tyna and return to town with her when Vince was settled in. Haddon came back out front and nodded at Clint.

Interesting. Clint hadn't met him.

Not long after, Haines came rushing in and went to Haddon. They started getting excited and a little loud. Clint heard, "... here too! What in hell's going on?! We can't...." and Haddon told Haines to lower his voice. They soon went out together.

"Our pot's beginning to boil, I think," Sergio noted. Clint grinned. They waited until Haddon and Haines had time to be by the China and leisurely got up to stroll toward the Bahia. They passed Judi and Canter, who were just going into the Grand Muralla. Canter seemed upset, and Judi called, "Hi, Clint! We're going to get some Chinese! Tell Tyna I'll try to get some of that sauce Ben makes for her. Caio!"

That meant something big was up with her that she didn't want Canter to know about. She pointed toward the Bahia with her thumb when she turned around to go into the restaurant.

Sergio and Clint walked toward the hotel, slowly. Clint suddenly pulled Sergio into the Grand Kahuna Hostal. "They're coming from back there. I think they went to Haddon's room. That may mean they have a gun or something."

"Haddon's staying at the Laguna. I suppose they might have," Sergio replied. "Perhaps we should go out the side door and be at the Bahia before they get there. A moment please."

He took out his radio and asked Emilio where Goode was. The Reef.

"This could get bad," Sergio warned. "Are you armed?"

"No. I never carry, around here."

"Be careful! Let's go the back way and to the hotel. They'll check there."

They went as fast as was reasonable along the back road and crossed to the Bahia Hotel as Haddon and Haines were coming down the steps to go directly toward the Reef, almost across the street. Clint and Sergio were about twenty steps behind them, but they didn't turn around to see them. They went to the restaurant entrance and stood, looking over the customers. Haines pointed to Goode, who was sitting at a table on the far side, close to the water. Emilio suddenly appeared beside them, and Sergio told him to go to Goode's table as quickly as possible and ask him for ID or something. Emilio nodded, and went to the table as Haddon and Haines got there. Goode was looking surprised as they came close. Haines had started to say something when Emilio said, "Excuse, please. Mr. Goode? Are you Mr. Goode?"

"Me? Er, yes? What's the problem?"

"There was a message at policia. It is to tell you

that a woman named Alice wishes to contact you with a thing importante.”

“Oh. Thank you. Alice who?”

“No, I think it was Alice Kansas.”

“Er, thank you. I don’t know any Alice Kansas. I’ll call at police headquarters after I have my dinner, if that is alright?”

“Yes, that is sufficient.”

“I have a bit of a surprise for your Mr. Haddon,” Sergio said. “Wait.”

He strolled up to the table and asked Emilio if Goode was a Mr. Haddon.

“No. This is Mr. Goode. I have the message from the desk.” (In Spanish.)

“Do you know who is this Mr. Haddon?”

“I’m Francis Haddon,” Haddon said. “What do you want?”

“I want to know why you produced a passport at the hostal that is not the one you produced at the airport, Mr. Haddon. Do you carry two passports?”

Haddon looked trapped. “I have a passport from France, and one from the United States. Perhaps I showed the wrong passport to the people at the hostal. I’m sure it will be a little nothing issue, officer.”

“Nothing? When you used the French passport to enter the country, where you declared nine thousand five hundred dollars efectivo, then used the US passport to enter through Paso Canoas, where you also declared nine thousand five hundred dollars efectivo?

"You never left the country on your French passport. How did you then come from Costa Rica a day later?

"You will come with Emilio. We will settle this question at the police station.

"You, sir. What is your name, and how do you know Mr. Haddon?"

"Er, we're from the same area in the states. I met him the other night at the Toro Loco bar. I'm Jerrald Haines."

"You knew Mr. Haddon in the united states? And did you, Mr, er, Goode, wasn't it? Know these people from the United States?"

"Yes. We're all from the same small town, and found it an amazing coincidence that so many from there are here at the same time. I was told that another person from the town is here."

"It is strange, but many strange things seem to happen here," Sergio said. "Well, please have a pleasant stay here. I'm sure this thing can be soon straightened out without causing too much inconvenience. People who carry two passports should not have them in the same place, or there is certain to be a question or twenty asked.

Particularly when both were used to enter the country in different places, and neither was used to leave the country."

"Well, that is, I think I'll go to the hotel now. I, er, I only wanted to say hello to Mr. Goode. We were, uh, friends back home, some years ago!"

"Very well." Sergio replied.

Haines left the table quickly, looking back over his shoulder as he got to the entrance. When he turned back, Clint was standing there. Haines looked like he'd been hit in the gut. Hard.

"Oh, hi! Haines, wasn't it? Did you see a police officer come in with a ... oh. There he is! Hope you enjoyed the meal. The food's good here. Caio!"

He went into the restaurant. Haines looked like his legs would collapse. He'd seen Sergio and Clint at the Grill, so knew something was wrong, if Clint was acting like he didn't think he'd been seen there. Clint smirked to himself. Emilio came toward the entrance with Haddon, who was looking very sick. Clint waved and went on to Sergio and Goode.

"Clint Faraday, Mr. Goode," Sergio introduced.

"Call me Ken. Both of you," Goode replied. "What's going on here? Why are all of us here together?

"I'm not objecting! I'm getting a very nice paid

vacation out of it! I think I love this place!"

"Vince Lasko and Louise Canter are here, too," Clint replied. "Give you a hint?"

"Yes. All that stuff about the Catholic priests or whatever and young children on the news. The church wasn't involved there. None of us are Catholic. It's in the past. We want it to stay."

"Do you know how many people have been murdered because of that?" Clint asked.

He looked shocked. "Murdered? I don't...?"

"Annie was the first. Longshire killed her. They know Vince has some evidence that will hang him and tie the whole sick bunch into the pedophile thing."

"I wondered about Annie. Longshire was right there? She chased her dog in front of a car? I don't know of anything else that happened that was connected."

"Landrow?" Clint asked.

"No. He was with his whole family. Longshire wasn't there. That had to be an accident ... though Landy was a good swimmer. I think he ate too much and went in the water and got cramps. The police declared that was the most likely thing. Nobody was there except his family."

"Including Uncle Ford?"

There as a long silence. "His own nephew?"

"It looks like it. Nephew or not, he knew too

much, and he had evidence hidden," Sergio said.

"But ... Landy never ... I mean ... what...?"

"I think he intended to blackmail Ford, which meant the whole bunch of them," Clint answered. "Did you ever see any evidence of that?"

"No, but Landy did say he could get anything he wanted from Ford. He did get money from him, sometimes."

Canter stormed into the restaurant and up to the table to demand, "Kenneth! Do not say one word to these people! They arrested Francis! They're trying to trap us!"

Judi came behind her and whispered to Clint, "I think your pot is about to boil over!"

"Us? What do you mean? It has very little to do with us, it has to do with the Cat Club. I have no great love for any of that bunch. I've seen what they did to a couple of people. They've ruined lives. We're much stronger than some others, Lou. We're a bit perverted, by nature, and it doesn't really affect our later lives, to any extent."

"They didn't do anything we didn't want, and you know it!" she screeched.

"You and me? I agree. Some others, no way! Look at Andy! He's been in and out of mental institutions for ten years! Look at Phyllis! She's a drunken dyke! *They* did that to them, and *you* know *that*!"

"We may have hit the jackpot here," Sergio whispered to Clint.

"We didn't do anything that we didn't want to do!" she insisted.

"We didn't. We aren't the only ones there. I was always a little bi. It hasn't bothered me to admit it. I wasn't made that way, I was born that way. You aren't a sex addict because of them, you were born to be. We're the most common types they attract, but they forced some into things that made a mess out of their lives. John Gilden wasn't a natural homo. He's living that life now, and is miserable. You and I don't know how many are like that. We haven't been around them for years. They've kept on doing the same things. I'm not about to protect them."

"But, it's not, I mean, we can't...."

"Do you know that Annie was pushed in front of that car by Longshire? Did you know Ford killed Landy? Do you know how many others were murdered by them?"

She looked shocked. "Annie was my friend!" she cried. "Oh, dear God! It can't be true!"

"It is."

"Well, that was interesting," Judi said. "Louise is a nympho, and knows it. She's having fun. Her only problem is she thinks there's going to be a lot of trouble because some politicians can shut up everyone. When I told her there seemed to be some murders, she got really scared. She says she was never connected in any way to anything like that. She's most torn up because she and Annie used to trade secrets.

"What's the next step? You can't do anything about that here. It was there in the states."

"We can. We will," Sergio promised. "We can give them a lot of incontrovertible evidence that Longshire killed Annie. There's no statute of limitations on murder, and it doesn't matter one whit that he's a bigshot politician."

"He's not, anymore," Manny, who had joined them for breakfast, said. "He declined to run last year for personal reasons. I think he feels the noose is getting a bit tight now."

"We can get the whole ring who are in it now. As Canter and Goode agree, they didn't stop back before the statute of limitations kicked in," Clint replied. "Look at what Haines and Canter were saying at the Toro Loco. He hasn't stopped. I wish we could get a couple of the kids to testify here."

"We don't bother with that with the street kids. Like Goode said, they like it, and they don't do anything they don't want to do," Emilio said.

"But the law is still there, on the books," Judi pointed out. "You don't have to be pragmatic and practical, you can act like they were your own kids and bury those slimewad bastards!"

"No. Leave the kids here out of it," Clint said.

"If the states won't act, I'll see they get a lot of international attention," Sergio promised.

"We have a crew who're investigating the way our organization investigates," Manny added. "It's not like the old days. We have the clue about the cat'seye ring, and can use that to bring a lot of attention by our people to anyone who sported that little item. One out of fifty will be innocent. We'll determine that. I intend to see every one of those bastards are caught and prosecuted. Pedophiles don't fare too well in prison."

"You'd act to help the law?" Sergio asked, with a grin. Manny had helped numerous times.

"I'm a father. That makes a huge difference in the way a man looks at things."

"We have to tie this thing together, then tie it

around a few necks," Clint suggested.

"What do you know! That worked!" Emilio cried, getting the finger from Clint.

They discussed it a bit more, then Clint and Sergio went to the airport to meet Robert Dobbs. They wondered what he was going to be like. It was possible that Goode would testify. It wasn't likely Canter would.

They stopped by the cells to see how Haddon was faring. He seemed resigned to the fact he would be deported. He didn't have a clue as to what was really up. They could hold him for as long as they liked here, because of the passport laws. He'd tried to bribe two different people. It would have worked if Sergio hadn't made it plain that this was a serious matter and not some way to rip some gringo off for a few bucks. Anybody who accepted a bribe from anyone in this case was going to serve at least the minimum sentence for taking a bribe: 4 years.

Clint felt evil. "Do you know a Robert Dobbs from your little town?" he asked.

"Bobbie Dobbs? What's he got to do with anything? He's been on some kind of rant against a couple of people for years. He's a nutcase."

"We're going to meet him at the airport."

"Fuck!" He turned his back, and wouldn't say anything more. Clint and Sergio went on out and took the police truck to the airport. "I think it's dawning on friend Haddon that this isn't about two passports at all. We don't give a damn about that kind of thing, unless it's tied to something else," Sergio noted. Clint gave him a high five.

"Ah! There he is. My god! He looks like that preacher who people were following around to find the art!"

"He does look pious as unholy hell, doesn't he?" Clint agreed. "Emanuel turned out to be okay or better."

"We can but hope. The information on him didn't mention religion."

They waited at baggage checkout, and told Dobbs they'd take him to the Olas. It was on their way, and they wanted to talk to him.

"Lou called me. It's about the old sex thing? Someone was murdered? Annie? Even Landy?"

"It looks like it," Sergio answered. "We have to get what evidence we can to present to the US. We've already talked with Haddon, Haines, Goode, Lasko, and Canter.

"It's to tag Longshire and his little club for murder and worse."

"Haddon and Haines are part of the club."

"We know. Lasko and Goode will probably help. Canter might, but I doubt it," Clint said.

"I'll tell you a story. You can decide whether or not I'll testify, in a heartbeat!"

"Oh? You one of them whose life is fucked up by them?"

"They only raped me and gave me AIDS. You figure it!"

"Why didn't you report it?!" Sergio cried.

"I did. It was under investigation for a couple of years, and they couldn't get enough evidence to take it to court. The prosecutor, some guy named Longshire, continued it until it died."

"Longshire killed Annie. We can pretty much prove it," Sergio explained. "Your testimony will clinch it!"

"Get ready for a long and detailed statement," he said. "I've learned a few things. I just can't prove them. I have names and dates. I've done a little investigating on my own."

"I have some influence in certain things in the states. I can guarantee the investigation will be intense and dead, and I use the term under advice, accurate," Clint promised.

"Let's get it done! I intend to have a great vacation one time before I die, and this is my opportunity! I just wish there were some girls I could enjoy it with!"

"There are. I know three very sexy and nice girls who have SIDA. If you have it, you won't be giving it to someone else who has it."

"So. I might live another eight months to a year. It's late, but I *did* find paradise!"

They took him to the hotel and checked him in. He then went to the police station and to the corregidor, who wouldn't touch it, then back to the police station, where Dobbs gave a very long and very detailed statement and directions for getting a box of files he'd collected, along with photographs ("Ford got me interested in candid photography. I have a few things that may shock hell out of even you!") he didn't dare show to Longshire and his cohorts. He was there until after ten PM. Seven hours.

He then went to the Olas to clean up and go out for the night. Estefan would stay close at all times. Those people would be getting desperate now.

Clint went home to his wife.

"Well, we have some reports," Manny said, as they sat around a table at El Ultimo Refugio for the famous Mahi-Mahi. "My investigators found twenty three of the twenty six in the ring. The others won't stay out of it for long. We turned it over to the state, and brought the national court and FBI into it, because they've acted in several states and in foreign countries. The organization owns enough judges and top cops that we can guarantee they aren't going to get away with it. This bunch will be prosecuted to the top. It's going to get big, fast!"

"I heard four people committed suicide who would have been prosecuted. Big deal rich businessmen," Judi said. "Remember that CIA man who got sick of what he was supposed to be doing and retired here? His wife can get all kinds of things."

"Know any names?" Manny asked.

"A Boomerson and a Georges and maybe a Sonisorn, but that could have been a legitimate accident."

"Boomerson? That's one we couldn't locate.

Yet," Manny said.

"Well, Haines and Haddon are caught and fighting extradition for all they're worth, but we had some testigos who were given immunity because of their age to testify that the two of them felt them up and tried to get them to do all those disgusting things their father warned them about," Estefan said smugly.

"Oh, come on! No one ever warned them about anything like that here!" Judi cried.

"Well, all we have is their sworn testimony that was backed up by placing the accused with small children at times testified to. No one would refute a single word of it, though some refused to confirm, either."

"Longshire is facing the chair, while Blanton is facing the gas chamber. There will be others who will face a lot worse fate. Pedophiles do not fare well in prison, and the minimum sentence anywhere is nine years. All-in-all, it was a thing that turned out much better than I would have believed when we started this," Emilio said. "Vince should be safe enough. He can have friends now, without worrying that they'll get murdered."

"I think I like Panamá more than anyplace I've been," Vince replied. "I'll probably spend about half the year here and half traveling. I like the open lifestyle."

"I like the openness, too," Lou said. "They won't let me stay. I have to leave in another three months, but I'll be back."

"I have to leave next week. They won't allow people with AIDS to stay here long. I don't blame them," Dobbs said. "I know how I'd feel if there was someone around my family who had AIDS, even if I would be most careful."

"You're a rare exception to the ones we get, sometimes," Sergio explained. "We've had some few here who, it turned out, would deliberately try to infect others. What we call a revenge complex. The trouble is, they would infect people who didn't have anything to do with their problem. Some of them got it from that type."

"I know. I was talking to one of the girls who said she had a girlfriend who has it and is still a whore at the local bars. She doesn't warn anyone.

"I agree with your friend, Dave. He says that kind should get a bullet between the eyes. It's attempted murder one, at the very best. Save your sympathy for someone who deserves it. He thinks the sex thing shouldn't be tied to an age number with the boys. It shouldn't with the girls, except the boys aren't going to end up pregnant, and the girls would. He agrees that the Indio kids know most of what they have to know about sex, and handle it very well. It might be alright if they want it, but trying to force anything on them shouldn't be tolerated at all. He's just glad he's never been attracted to kids. He liked women around thirty when he was seventeen and likes woman around their thirties, now that he's in his seventies.

"We all like things that whatever causes it attracts us to."

"Yes. I like a woman with a big ass. Dave and Clint are turned off by a big ass. That's why all women don't look alike. Everybody has his own fantasies. It's true with the women, too. I look at guys I think of as really a turnoff to women, then a bunch of women will think they're sexy as hell.

"Why all this?" Vince asked.

"The case is about sex. When you start thinking about sex, it gets deeper and deeper," Tyna said. "I like men like Clint. I've been in love with him since I was twelve. Most never get the one who's perfect for them. I lucked out!"

"Yeah! What're you going to name your first kid?" Judi asked. "Throckmorton?"

"Well, we considered that, but Clint wants a name that's a little easier to remember. He likes Beverly," Tyna shot back.

"That's an English name!" Sergio protested. "He needs an Indio name. How about Smitty?"

"Nah! Too Australian," Emilio said. "How about Mario?"

"No. Too Italian. Hm. How about Ahmad?" Manny suggested.

"No. Too black. How about Gaylord? If he's gay, that would be perfect!" Estefan said.

"Vic. If it's a girl, Viki," Clint said.

"You stay out of this! You're just the father! You can't name the kid!" Lou said. "How about my name? Lou? It could be a boy or girl, and wouldn't make a difference."

"Excuse me, but have you seen my son, Cole?" a woman asked. "He's supposed to be here. He's thirteen, and I'm afraid he'll get in trouble. There are you police officers here. He's a gringo, like me. He's blond and blue-eyed. I'm so afraid for him!"

"Don't be," Lou counseled. "He'll probably only get laid by some local girl. Blond and blue-eyed turns the natives on like you won't believe!"

The woman was looking shocked. "He's too young for all that!" she cried.

"Oh, grow up! The boys out front are ten and twelve, and've been getting laid since they were eight. The people here don't treat anyone that age like a little child. He's probably been having sex for years already, and you don't even know it," Lou lectured. "It's a vacation. Let the kid have some fun."

"I was a late-bloomer in the states," Clint said. "I was thirteen, the first time.

"I like that. Cole is a good name."

The woman was really shocked, now. "Don't worry. We're just having fun. Your son is in no danger here," Sergio said. "The police keep a close eye out for anything. We just aren't obvious about it."

She looked uncertain, then grinned. She said maybe she was overprotective, but things were different in the states. Believe it or not, you had to keep even very young children in sight at all times, in public. Horrible things could happen.

"We know," Vince said. It was the understatement of the year, but he managed to keep a straight face.

C. D. Moulton's works are available on most major outlets as printed or e-books. CD writes the CD Grimes, PI mysteries, the Det. Lt. Nick Storie mysteries, the Clint Faraday mysteries, the Flight of the Maita science fiction series, books on orchid culture and many others of many types. Mystery, adventure, intrigue, science fiction, fantasy, para-normal, mild erotica, and factual.